Lucy's ⸻

Mary has been writing books for children and teenagers for fifteen years, and has now had more than 50 titles published. She writes funny stories, animal stories, spooky stories and romantic stories, and before she started *Lucy's Farm* she spent some time in Devon to be sure she got all the details right. Mary has two grown-up children and lives just outside London in a small Victorian cottage. She has a cat called Maisie and a collection of china rabbits. She says her favourite hobby is "pottering", as this is when she gets most of her ideas.

Titles in the LUCY'S FARM series

1. A Lamb for Lucy
2. Lucy's Donkey Rescue
3. Lucy's Badger Cub
4. A Stormy Night for Lucy
5. Lucy's Wild Pony
6. Lucy's Perfect Piglet

All of the LUCY'S FARM books can be ordered at
your local bookshop or are available by post
from Book Service by Post (tel: 01624 675137).

LUCY'S FARM

Lucy's Perfect Piglet

Mary Hooper

Illustrations by Anthony Lewis

MACMILLAN CHILDREN'S BOOKS

First published 2000 by Macmillan Children's Books
a division of Macmillan Publishers Limited
25 Eccleston Place, London SW1W 9NF
Basingstoke and Oxford
www.macmillan.com

Associated companies throughout the world

ISBN 0 330 36799 4

Text copyright © Mary Hooper 2000
Illustrations copyright © Anthony Lewis 2000

The right of Mary Hooper to be identified as the
author of this work has been asserted by her in accordance
with the Copyright, Designs and Patents Act 1988.

1 3 5 7 9 8 6 4 2

A CIP catalogue record for this book is available from
the British Library

Phototypeset by Intype London Ltd
Printed and bound in Great Britain by Mackays of Chatham plc, Kent

Chapter One

"Don't you dare!" Lucy's mum said to her. "Every single one of those cakes has been counted."

Lucy sighed as she looked at the racks on which sponge fingers with lemon icing and slices of sugared apple cake were cooling. "You've been doing nothing but baking cakes for *weeks*," she complained to her mum. "I haven't been allowed to eat a thing!"

Julie Tremayne tucked a wisp of hair behind her ears and sighed. Lucy's mum was a tall, pretty woman with Lucy's

1

blonde colouring and, this morning, a rather harassed expression. "That's because I want to have a full stall at the fête this afternoon," she said. "If I let you lot start on them, half the cakes will have disappeared before I've even got them there."

"I bet you've got hundreds more in the freezer!" Lucy said.

Lucy Tremayne, her mum, dad and little sister Kerry lived at Hollybrook Farm, in a village called Bransley, in the Devon countryside. The family ran a dairy herd with about fifty Friesian cows, including Buttercup – Lucy's special cow. Lucy had helped at the birth of Daisy, Buttercup's calf, one stormy night. The Tremaynes also had some sheep and a donkey, Donald, that Lucy had rescued from the beach. As well as these they had Roger and Podger, the cross-bred collie dogs, a selection of cats and a clutch of chicks and chickens. Lucy was always looking for more animals to collect. The more they had on the farm the better she liked it!

"Now, the Bed and Breakfast man said he wouldn't be here until five or six o'clock because he has several other places to visit first," Lucy's mum said. She counted on her fingers. "The fête starts at one-thirty and I should have sold out by four o'clock, so I can pack up and be back here easily by five."

"Bed and Breakfast man? Someone else is coming to stay?" Lucy asked. Her mum took in paying guests to help with the farm expenses, and that summer they'd been quite busy with holiday-makers and people wanting weekend breaks. At the moment they had a Mr and Mrs Walker staying for two weeks, but the couple had gone to visit friends in Cornwall that day. Just as well, Lucy thought, with everything else that was going on.

Julie Tremayne shook her head. "No, not a guest. You haven't been listening, Lucy. This is the *inspector*!"

"Oh, yes," Lucy said, remembering that her mum had been going on about the farm being assessed for the tourist board's *Best Bed and Breakfast* brochure.

From underneath the scrubbed pine table, a podgy hand crept up to take a sponge cake. "No you don't, Kerry!" Lucy Tremayne said. Removing the cake from Kerry's grasp, she moved the rack along the table and out of her toddler daughter's way.

"It's hard times, Kerry," Lucy said to her little sister. "No lovely home-made stuff for us. You and I could starve to death for all Mum cares!" She looked at her mum. "Where's the inspector coming from?"

"From Honley Tourist Board," her mum said. Honley was their nearest big town. "He's going to inspect us for this year's book. If he likes us we'll get a four-crown rating – and if he doesn't, we won't get in there at all."

Lucy pulled a face. "What's he going to be looking at?"

"Everything! The two bedrooms we use for the guests, the bathroom, the sitting room – and then he's going to have supper with us." Julie Tremayne rolled her eyes.

"So everything's got to be neat, tidy and absolutely clean."

"I'll try and keep Podger out of the butter dish then," Lucy said. As her mum gave a shriek, she added, "Well, at least we know he's coming and can make a special effort. It'd be awful if he just turned up without telling us."

"Yes, but why did he have to come *today*!" her mum wailed. "There's the fête, and Mr and Mrs Walker wanting supper tonight, and the sheep to be sheared and *everything*!" She looked at her watch. "It's already nine-thirty and your dad's not back for his breakfast. That's going to hold me up."

"I expect he's gone straight down to the paddock to see the sheep shorn," Lucy said. "He won't have time to come in for breakfast." She looked at her mum innocently. "Shall I take him a couple of cakes?"

"Certainly not! You can take him a bacon sandwich," said her mum. She picked up Kerry and hoisted the toddler onto her hip. "I'll make you one to take down to him. But before I do that I'll get my cakes out of the freezer. If I don't, my customers will be breaking their teeth on frozen rock buns."

"Rock buns!" Lucy said. "My favourites!"

But her mum went out to the big freezer in the pantry, pretending not to hear.

Lucy was just leaving the farmhouse with her dad's breakfast sandwich in a greaseproof bag, when she heard a familiar bleating coming from further down the lane. As she opened the five-bar gate which led out of the farmyard a small sheep galloped around the corner as if a hundred foxes were on its tail. "*Baaabaaa!*"

"Rosie!" Lucy said. "Whatever's the matter with you?"

Rosie ran into Lucy and stopped dead. The baa-ing ceased.

Stowing the bacon sandwich safely inside her jacket, Lucy bent down to fuss the little sheep, running her fingers through the thick creamy fleece. Lucy had hand-raised Rosie since the sheep was a couple of hours old, feeding her through the night with a bottle, and Rosie seemed to think Lucy was her own mum.

"What is it then?" Lucy asked again – and then, from the paddock, she heard the loud buzzing noise which said the sheep-shearer was at work. She patted Rosie. "I get it," she said. "You don't want to lose all your fleece, do you? You're frightened of the machine."

Shutting the gate behind them, Lucy began to walk down the lane. Happy to be close to Lucy, Rosie trotted beside her.

Because she was only a sheep, she'd already forgotten what she'd been in such a state about.

"You might not like the noise it makes and it *is* a bit tickly – not that I've ever been shorn myself – but you'll like it when you haven't got that thick, matted fur coat on. Especially when it's really hot. And all the other sheep are being shorn. You don't want to look out of fashion, do you?"

Chatting away to Rosie, Lucy walked to the paddock. The noise of the clipping machine had stopped by the time she got there, and Lucy saw her dad was leaning on the fence and talking to Mr Oakley, the travelling shearing man. The sheep yet to be done were running round in their little enclosure within the paddock, and Roger and Podger were lying in wait, hoping a sheep was going to leap the hedge so they could round it up.

Four sheep, their fleeces cropped very

short, were standing in the paddock munching grass. Lucy laughed when she saw them. "Don't they look funny! No wonder Rosie ran away. She didn't want to look like that!"

Lucy's dad, Tim Tremayne, was a tall, well-built man who had a year-round tan and a ready grin. "I knew that Rosie would come up to find you," he said, "so I called Podger off and let her go."

Lucy gave her dad his sandwich, then said hello to Mr Oakley, who was old and weather-beaten, with a grey curly beard. She opened the gate for Rosie to go into the paddock with the others. "There you go. In with your friends," she said.

"You haven't brought a flask of coffee down with you, have you?" her dad asked, munching his bacon sandwich.

Lucy shook her head. "Didn't think of it," she said, "and Mum certainly didn't. She's knee-deep in rock buns and apple cake for the fête." As her dad raised his eyebrows hopefully she added, "And don't bother to look hopeful. She wouldn't give Kerry as much as a *currant*, let alone us."

Her dad laughed. "Tell you what, now you're here to keep an eye on this lot, I'll go back and get myself a drink."

"I can't stay here! I've got to get Donald ready to give donkey rides at the fête!" Lucy said.

"Plenty of time for that!" her dad said cheerily. He patted her on the back. "I won't be long, love." Whistling for the dogs to come by, he started back to the farmhouse.

Lucy sighed. She had to groom Donald thoroughly and polish his saddle ready for him to give rides for a couple of hours. She didn't really have time to stay with the sheep.

"So you're in charge, then!" Mr Oakley said.

"It looks like it." Lucy leaned over the fence. "Can you do Rosie next, please?" She pointed. "*That* one. She might not mind it so much now that I'm around." Lucy hesitated, "You'll be careful with her, won't you?"

Mr Oakley grinned. "I'll treat her like I would my own!"

Lucy smiled and then watched rather anxiously as he grabbed Rosie by the scruff of her neck, then expertly tipped her up so that she was almost lying on her back. Holding the sheep tightly between his legs, Mr Oakley took his shearing gun – which was a bit like a large electric razor – and began to run it expertly over her body.

Rosie wriggled and kicked her legs a bit, gave a couple of *baaaas* of shock and then went silent. A few moments later there was a fine sheepskin rug lying on the floor

– and Rosie was looking pink and bald
and rather surprised.

"Oh, Rosie!" Lucy said, and burst out
laughing. "You look like a sausage on
legs!"

Chapter Two

The sheep had all been shorn and Lucy was leading Donald back to the farmyard to be groomed when she caught sight of their neighbour, Mr Mackintyre, coming across his field towards her.

Mr Mackintyre – known to everyone as Mr Mack – was an old-style farmer who had a very large farm near the Tremaynes, with many acres of land and several hundred sheep. Lucy and he got on rather well – it was Mr Mack who'd helped rescue Donald from the beach, and he was also the one who'd persuaded Tim

14

Tremayne to buy Buttercup, Lucy's special little cow.

"Mr Mack! Coming to the fête?" Lucy called over to him. Last year Mr Mack had run a Guess the Weight of the Ram competition. "Do you want me to book a ride on Donald for you?" she joked.

But Mr Mack didn't seem to have heard her. Lucy called again, waiting in the lane with Donald for Mr Mack to join them. To her surprise though he suddenly turned round and started walking hurriedly back towards his own farm.

Lucy waved and called again, then gave up. "That's funny!" she said to Donald. "I'm sure he saw us. Why didn't he wave? Why did he turn back?"

Puzzled, she carried on to Hollybrook Farm. She let herself in through the gate and tethered Donald loosely in the small hay barn next to the house. Then she gathered all the equipment she was going to need to groom the donkey. She was going to wash his face, brush his coat and even trim his fringe, she decided. He was going to be the smartest donkey anyone had ever seen. The more children that rode on him, the more money Lucy would collect for the local children's hospital, which was the charity supported by the fête this year.

When Lucy went indoors, Kerry was in the boot lobby sitting in Roger's basket, while both dogs were squashed together in the other basket. Lucy took off her boots and jacket and went through to the kitchen. Her mum and dad were standing on each side of the table, looking rather worried – although Lucy didn't really notice this. What she did notice was the table, which was groaning under a huge selection of different cakes – rock buns, oatie biscuits, flapjacks, caramel short-breads, and an oval china plate piled high with pink sugar pigs.

16

"Oh – I didn't know you'd made sugar pigs!" Lucy said. "Aren't they beautiful!"

She put out her hand to take one, but her mum automatically pushed it away.

"Dear little noses and eyes . . . and they've even got string tails!" Lucy said. "I thought you hated pigs, Mum!"

"I do," her mum said, rather absently, "but I don't hate sugar ones."

"How did you make their tails curl?"

"Curling tongs," her mum said, and then she looked out of the window and gave a great sigh.

Lucy's dad still hadn't spoken. He just stood there.

"The sheep are finished," Lucy told him. "Mr Oakley's going to bring the fleeces up and he wants you to settle the bill with him."

"OK," her dad said. "Are the sheep all done?"

"I just told you they were!" Lucy said in surprise. Suddenly anxious, she looked from her dad to her mum. "What's the matter? Why are you both just standing there looking at each other?"

"You'd better tell her," Lucy's mum said.

"Tell me what?" Lucy felt a cold shiver run over her. "What's happened?"

Her dad held up an envelope. "It's this. We've just received a letter from the local council."

Lucy looked at him, mystified. What was all this about?

"It's from the planning authority," Lucy's mum explained. "It says that Mr Mack is selling his farm to a firm of developers."

"What does *that* mean?"

"Well, the developers want to build on his land. Build lots of houses."

Lucy still didn't really understand.

All she knew was that her mum and dad were looking more worried than she'd ever seen them look before. "I still don't—"

"The developers have applied for permission to build on the land," her dad said, his voice impatient and anxious. "They want to put a big estate of houses there. We'd have five hundred homes right on our doorstep!"

Lucy gasped. "But what would happen to us?"

"We'd be overwhelmed. We'd have traffic up and down outside our door all day, and the cows' summer field would be surrounded by houses on three sides. Farming would be well-nigh impossible!"

"And who'd want to have bed and breakfast in the middle of a housing estate?" Lucy's mum added grimly.

Lucy looked at her mum and dad, stunned. So *that* was why Mr Mack hadn't wanted to speak to her. "But how could he do something like that?" she said to her dad. "Mr Mack's lived on that farm ever since he was born. Doesn't he care about it? Doesn't he care about us?"

Her mum sighed. "It's all down to money, love. He wants to sell the farm, and his land will be worth an awful lot more if they build on it."

"But can't we persuade him not to sell? Can't we speak to him?"

"I just did," her dad said with a short, rather bitter laugh. "I rang him a moment ago. Oh, he was very embarrassed. Said he'd been trying to find a way to tell us before the authorities did, but hadn't managed to get round to it. I'm afraid I gave him a piece of my mind."

Lucy clenched her fists. Their farm. *Her animals*! "I'll tell him too," she said. "He needn't think I'm going to be friends with him any more!"

"I'm afraid it won't do any good, love," her mum said. "He's already made up his mind. He told your dad he's had enough of farming – that he's just not making enough profit."

"None of us are making what we used to," Lucy's dad said feelingly. "But to get rid of his farm . . ."

21

"I'd never have thought it of him," Lucy's mum said sadly.

"Nor would I," said Lucy. Never in a million years had she thought her friend, Mr Mack, would betray them.

As they got ready for the fête, every member of the family was very subdued. Even Kerry seemed to sense the atmosphere and wasn't as bright and bouncy as usual. Lucy put the finishing touches to Donald and tied ribbons on his bridle, while her mum packed the Land Rover with all her cakes, then gave the house a last-minute clean and tidy-up ready for the Tourist Board man.

"At least no one's here to dirty the place this afternoon," Julie Tremayne said with satisfaction, putting a jug of flowers in the kitchen window. "It'll stay clean and tidy all day."

At one o'clock Lucy's mum and Kerry

set off in the Land Rover and Lucy followed with Donald. Lucy's dad had said he'd join them later when he'd repaired the fence in the lower field.

The fête, which opened at one-thirty, was being held in the spacious gardens of the Tregarth-Bartons' house – the biggest house in the village. There was a tea marquee, a pet zoo, some small fairground rides for the younger children and lots of stalls selling country wares. Brightly coloured flags and lights were hung around the old walls, while loudspeakers played music and made announcements about the various competitions.

Lucy found her space straight away. RIDE ON DONALD THE DONKEY! OLD-FASHIONED FUN FOR THE UNDER TWELVES! it said on a painted banner hung across an apple tree. Lucy took her place underneath the sign feeling anxious and fluttery in her tummy. What was going to happen to Hollybrook Farm? She'd already heard Mrs Tregarth-Barton say that it was "shocking news about the housing estate" and she'd seen her mum, looking worried, deep in conversation with several people. Just wait until she saw Mr Mack, that was all. *She'd* tell him . . .

Lucy tethered Donald to the tree and walked around a bit before the fête opened, looking at all the stalls, making up her mind what to go on and keeping an eye open for Mr Mack.

But his GUESS THE WEIGHT OF THE RAM stall was empty. No sturdy ram with curling horns had appeared, and there was no Mr Mack in his tweedy suit carrying a clipboard and shouting at everyone to come and have a go.

Right next to where he should have been, though, was something which made Lucy stop in her tracks. BOWLING FOR A PIG the banner said, and on a table at the front of the stall was a small wooden crate, lined with straw. In this crate were eight piglets, some curled round snugly asleep, some wriggling and squeaking. Lucy noticed one with a black spot on his left ear. He was especially cute.

"Oh!" Lucy cried, peering in. "Isn't he *lovely*!" Lucy loved piglets, and this one was plump and puppy-sized, his tiny curly tail sticking up.

The stall-holder, Mrs Bessant, who farmed just outside the village, smiled at Lucy. "Want to win one? They're eight weeks old and eating proper food."

Lucy beamed. "Yes, please! What do I have to do?"

Mrs Bessant pointed behind her, where a long runway stretched right back to the garden wall. At the far end, ten skittles had been set up. "It's just like a bowling alley," she said. "You get three balls, and if you can score twenty-five you win piggy-wig here."

From further down the gardens came a shout from Lucy's mum on her cake stall. "Don't you dare!" she called across to Lucy. "We don't want any horrid pigs!"

Mrs Bessant laughed. "It doesn't sound as if your mum would be very keen."

"She hates pigs!" Lucy said. "She says they're dirty – but I know they're not!" she added hastily.

"Farmers' wives are used to dirt," Mrs Bessant said. "There must be more to it than that."

Lucy nodded. "She told me that when she was really little, she was walking through a farmyard when a pig jumped up at her and knocked her over. She's never liked them since." Lucy glanced up at Mrs Bessant. "I'll have a go later, though," she said. "I'm not going to win, because I've never bowled before."

"You do that," Mrs Bessant said. "It's all for a good cause."

Lucy looked at the piglet with the black spot on its tiny ear and stroked it. "Though you're a real darling and I'd really love to win *you* . . ."

Chapter Three

"Well done, love!" Mrs Bessant beamed. "Fifteen skittles down in two balls!"

Lucy stared down the runway at the scattered skittles in surprise. What a fluke – she'd never bowled in her life before. But – somehow – she seemed to be good at it.

A small crowd of onlookers surrounded Lucy and, beside her, her best friend Bethany Brown was holding Donald. The donkey had completed his two-hour riding stint, which was all Lucy thought he should do, and she'd been just about to take him home when she'd remembered the piglets. She and Beth had come across to have a go, only to discover there was just one piglet left to win – the one with the spot on its ear. Beth had gone first but only managed to knock over two skittles with her three balls. Now Lucy was surprising everyone.

"Go for it, Lucy!" Beth called. "Win that piglet!"

Lucy looked over her shoulder across the field. Luckily, her mum was fully occupied on her cake stall, and hadn't noticed that her daughter was bowling to win the one animal in the world that she couldn't stand!

Lucy held the last wooden ball in the air. She wouldn't win . . . of course she wouldn't win. It was just a bit of fun.

She took three steps backwards then turned and ran forward, flinging the ball onto the runway with as much force as she could.

"Go, Lucy!" she heard Beth call.

The ball skewed sideways, then seemed to straighten itself and head right for the very centre of the set of skittles. Lucy held her breath as the ball crashed into the front skittle and, with a clatter, made all the others knock into each other. She closed her eyes for a moment – and then heard several shouts. When she opened her eyes she discovered that she'd knocked every single skittle over!

"Total score – twenty-five!" Mrs Bessant said, beaming all over her face. She winked at Lucy. "I had a feeling you'd win – that's why I saved him for you."

"Oh wow!" Beside her, Beth was jumping up and down. "You've won him. You've won the piglet!"

Lucy stared at Mrs Bessant in shock. "Oh!" she said. "I didn't really—"

But Mrs Bessant was bustling forward with a cardboard box in her hands. "Now," she said, "here's a nice sturdy box to take him home in. As I said, he's eight weeks old and he'll eat anything – potato peelings, bread, bits of meat. Mix it up with a bit of barley meal. He's been checked over by a vet and he's perfectly healthy. Don't worry about your mum – she'll love him when she sees him."

"But . . ." Lucy stuttered. But my mum really *hates* pigs, she wanted to say. And I've got nowhere to put him. And my dad will go mad if I come home with another animal.

But Mrs Bessant was picking up the piglet and putting him in a box with several handfuls of straw. "Enjoy him!" she said, handing him over. "If you've just got the one piglet you can teach him to do tricks, you know. He'll be just like a puppy!"

The people surrounding the stall looked at Lucy and smiled, and one or two glanced at the little piglet in the box and cooed at him, as if he were a baby.

"A little darlin', he is," Mrs Bessant said. "Have fun with him while he's a nipper, then you can feed him up to make a good few meals come next winter."

Lucy looked at her, horrified. As if she'd ever be able to *eat* him!

Stunned, she walked away, followed by Beth with Donald. "I don't believe what's just happened," she said to Beth in a shocked voice. "I never thought I'd *win*."

"It's not that bad, is it?" Beth said. "There must be somewhere on your farm you can hide him."

Lucy shook her head. "Not for long. And when they find him they'll go mad. If you knew how my mum goes on about pigs."

"What about your friend Mr Mack, then? He'll hide him for you."

Lucy shook her head. "He's not my friend any more," she said sadly, and was just going to tell Beth what Mr Mack had done when there was a high-pitched squealing from the box.

Both girls peered in and the piglet looked up at them through the straw, his little snout woffling up and down like a rabbit's.

"Oh, look!" Beth said. "Isn't he just the cutest, pinkest thing you've ever seen?"

"Yes, he is," Lucy said, looking at the blond fluff on the piglet's ears, his tiny dark eyes and the funny expression on his pink face. "He's absolutely gorgeous." She sighed. "And my mum's going to go absolutely mad."

Beth put her hand in to tickle the top of the pig's nose. "What are you going to call him?"

Lucy sighed again. "Trouble," she said.

Ten minutes later, Lucy was heading for home with Donald and the piglet. She'd met her dad on the way, but he'd been in such a hurry to get down to the fête for an hour or so and then back home for the afternoon milking, that he hadn't even noticed Lucy was carrying a cardboard box under her arm. Lucy decided that she could probably hide Trouble in the hay barn for a while until she had worked out how she was going to tell her mum and dad about him.

How were they going to react? Not well, she thought. Apart from the fact that her mum hated pigs, after the shock they'd had that morning they weren't exactly going to be in a good mood at finding they had an extra mouth to feed, a pig sty to buy and even more vet's bills to pay. At any other time, Lucy knew that Mr Mack would have helped her. But now? Well, she just wouldn't ask him.

Opening the gate that led to Hollybrook Farm, Lucy saw that Mr and Mrs Walker's car was back in the yard. And there was a small black car, too – one she'd never seen before.

She tied Donald up in the hay barn and went into the kitchen, the box under her arm, to find Mrs Walker making herself a cup of tea.

"Hello, dear." Mrs Walker, a large, pleasant elderly lady with silvery hair and very pink cheeks, held up the teapot. "I knew your mum wouldn't mind me making a cuppa."

"Of course not," Lucy said. The couple had already been there a week and Lucy's mum had told them to treat the farmhouse as if it were their own home. "But whose is that car in the yard?"

"Oh, it's the tourist board man," Mrs Walker said. "Nice young chap. Said he was expected."

"Oh no!" Lucy wailed. She looked at her watch – it wasn't even four o'clock yet. "He's miles too early! Between five and six o'clock, Mum said." She looked out of the window and round the farmyard. "Where's he gone now?"

Mrs Walker looked vague. "Just for a walkabout, I think." She smiled. "How was the fête? What have you got in that cardboard box?"

"Oh . . . er . . ." Lucy felt herself going red.

"There he is!" Mrs Walker saved Lucy having to make up a fib by suddenly pointing out of the window. "He's just coming through the gate."

Lucy gave a silent scream. All the things her mum had said about the inspection ran through her mind. Everything had to be

37

spick and span, there must be no mud on the floor, and Kerry had to be stopped from sleeping in the dog basket. There certainly shouldn't be a piglet in the kitchen! What would any inspector think about *that*?

She gulped. Well, she was just about to find out, because he was on his way indoors . . .

Chapter Four

Quickly, Lucy shoved the cardboard box onto the draining board behind her and stood in front of it, smiling brightly at the inspector. "I'm Lucy Tremayne," she said, "and I'm terribly sorry but my mum's still at the fête in the village."

The inspector wasn't what Lucy would call "young" – he was about fifty with a small moustache and a bald head. "So I hear," he said with a smile, "and I'm sorry for disturbing you so early. At my last port of call they all had chickenpox, though, so I couldn't visit. It put my schedule right out."

"Oh dear," Lucy said. Behind her, she was aware of Trouble moving around in his straw. There was a snuffling noise and she coughed to cover it. "Chickenpox," she said to gain time. "Just fancy. What a shame."

"Would you like a cup of tea, Inspector?" Mrs Walker offered. "I've just made a pot."

Lucy froze. She hoped he wouldn't have one; she just wanted him to go.

"Not for me, thank you," the man said, and inwardly Lucy sighed with relief. "My name's Jack Bourne, by the way. I don't want to inspect the house without Mr and Mrs Tremayne being here, so I think I'll take myself off to the village for what's left of the fête."

"Oh, good!" Lucy cried. Then, as they both looked at her curiously, she added,

"Good . . . er . . . idea. There's lots of stalls still open. Maybe you can win yourself a . . . a something."

"If I walk back up to the village I can get an idea of the surroundings of the farm too, and will be able to write something about Bransley itself," Mr Bourne said.

From behind Lucy came a scrabbling and a squeak.

"Ooh, what's that?" Mrs Walker said, and before Lucy could say anything she crossed the kitchen to peer into the box. "Oh, a p—"

"*Puppy*!" Lucy interrupted quickly. "Rather an unusual puppy. It's one of the . . . er . . . furless varieties." She quickly adjusted the straw over the piglet so that none of him could be seen.

Mrs Walker looked confused. "Well, if you say so, ducks, but it looks awfully like a p—"

Lucy flung her arm expansively around

the room. "Do you like the kitchen, Mr Bourne? We've got a dining room but everyone usually eats in here at this big table. There's a pantry this way. Come and see." Smiling madly, Lucy led the way over to the pantry. "We had a burglar once who shut me in here and I shouted and shouted and Rosie, my lamb, went to get help." She flung the door of the pantry open, struggling to think of something else to

say – anything to keep the inspector's attention away from the box on the draining board.

"Ah yes. A very nice pantry," Mr Bourne said, looking rather confused. "I like those old-fashioned jars and bottles on the shelves."

"Mum pickles her own onions, and beetroots, and—" Suddenly, glancing across the kitchen, Lucy saw the cardboard box wobbling. A small pink snout appeared over the edge, the box fell onto its side and Trouble ran out and along the worktop, his tiny feet clattering along the wood.

"Oh!" Mrs Walker cried.

"Look!" Lucy said desperately, pointing into the pantry. "There's eggs from our chickens – all nice and brown."

"Ah yes," Mr Bourne said, not sounding terribly interested.

"Have a closer look!" Lucy said

desperately. "Look at all those jars again! Some have got mulberry jam and some have got pickled onions and some have stewed gooseberries. See if you can see which is which!"

Leaving him standing there staring, looking rather bemused, Lucy dashed across the kitchen, scooped up Trouble, popped him back into the box and shoved the box inside the first cupboard she could find.

Mrs Walker was just standing there open-mouthed. "I've never seen a puppy that looked so much like a—"

Lucy smiled at her glassily. "Is your cup of tea all right?"

"I mean, are you *sure* it's a—"

"Aren't you going to take a cup to Mr Walker? I expect he'd like one." *Just go*, Lucy begged her silently.

Jack Bourne walked back from the pantry. "A very nice pantry. Very nice indeed. Now, as I said, I'll just pop down to the fête and maybe I'll meet up with your mum and dad while I'm down there."

Lucy dashed to the kitchen door to open it and usher him out. "Even if you don't, Mum said she'd be back by five," she said breathlessly. "And I expect Dad will be back to start the milking before that. Goodbye!"

"Goodbye," Mr Bourne said. "See you both later."

Lucy watched him walk across the farmyard and open the gate, then she got the cardboard box out of the cupboard and collapsed onto a chair. "*Phew*!"

Mrs Walker shook her head. "Now, what was that all about? Pigs and puppies indeed. What's going on here?"

Lucy looked up at her pleadingly. "Sorry, Mrs Walker. It *is* a piglet," she said. Delving into the straw, Lucy brought out Trouble and put him on the floor. The little piglet stared around him, then sniffed at one of the chair legs and began gnawing at it.

"I can see that," Mrs Walker said. "That is, unless they've started breeding puppies with snouts and curly tails."

She and Lucy stared down at Trouble, and he stopped nibbling and stared back at them. Then he gave a high-pitched squeal and began to run around the kitchen. He ran very fast and quite daintily, as if he was running on his toes.

Lucy and Mrs Walker both gave cries of delight.

"He runs like a dancer!" Lucy said.

"As if he's wearing high-heeled shoes!"

Trouble disappeared into a cupboard, just leaving a small pink bottom and a curly tail sticking out of the door.

"Isn't he gorgeous?" Lucy sighed. "I won him at the fair, you see, and because

Mum hates pigs – and what with the inspector coming and everything – I decided I'd have to hide him."

"So what are you going to do with him, ducks?" Mrs Walker asked.

Lucy shrugged. "I was going to hide him in the hay barn, but I think the inspector might want to look out there to make sure we haven't got rats or anything."

"Ooh, I hope not!" said Mrs Walker.

"No, course we haven't – the cats make sure of that," Lucy said. She frowned. "I think I might take him down to the woods. There are some old coops that Mr Mack used to keep pheasants in. I can hide young master Trouble away overnight with some straw and food, and then try and figure out what to do with him in the morning."

"That sounds a good idea."

"And Mrs Walker?"

"Yes, ducks?"

"Please don't say anything about him to Mum or Dad, will you? Not yet."

Mrs Walker winked. "It'll be our secret," she said.

Chapter Five

Lucy ran across a field towards the woods, cardboard box tucked under one arm. Inside, Trouble – having gobbled up two slices of bread and a cut-up apple – was fast asleep.

Stopping to get her breath back, Lucy looked in at him and couldn't stop herself letting out a long "Aaahhh". He looked so cute, fast asleep, lying on his back with his legs sticking straight out in front of him. If Mum could see you now, she thought, she'd *have* to love you.

Halfway across the field Lucy heard the

noise of a Land Rover and looked round. It was her dad, driving into the yard. He was back to do the milking – she'd got out just in time!

The farmhouse looked very pretty in the late afternoon sun, its stone walls glowing a soft gold and roses blooming around its door. As Lucy looked at it she thought sadly that soon, very soon, that view was going to change. There would be houses all around them – an estate of houses. Shops, even. She shook her head. The cows liked peace and quiet when they were being milked – it actually made them give more milk – but how were they going to get any peace with the constant roar of traffic up and down the lane? And it wouldn't be a lane any more, either, with wild flowers and raggedy hedgerows and animals looking over the gates. It would be a busy street, with yellow lamps and road markings and big signs. How awful . . .

Lucy continued across the field to Brockham Wood. Here, she knew, were Mr Mack's old pheasant coops. *Mr Mack*! It was all *his* fault that there were going to be so many horrible changes. She could hardly believe it of her old friend.

Lucy glanced at her watch. She'd just have time to put Trouble in one of the coops, settle him down, and get back to Hollybrook Farm by five. Then she'd get Donald back to the paddock, help her dad feed the sheep and see if her mum wanted any help with the evening meal. She was going to be very helpful indeed this evening, she decided. Anything her mum and dad needed doing was going to be done. And then, later, when the inspector had gone, she might gently bring up the subject of piglets.

"They'll love you when they see you,"

Lucy said to Trouble now, gently stroking the soft fluff on the piglet's back. Deep down, though, she wasn't quite so sure that they would . . .

Lucy entered the woods, trying to see through the trees. The pines grew close and tall at the edge of the wood and she blinked in the soft darkness, trying to remember exactly where the coops were.

Suddenly, as she was stepping across a mossy log, she heard a strange groan, like a wounded animal, and her heart leapt into her mouth. Was it an animal? Or was it a person – someone waiting to snatch her? Suddenly, she remembered her mum telling her never to go into the woods alone.

The groan came again – a long drawn-out moaning sound. Lucy stopped dead, pressed herself against a tree and kept as quiet as a mouse.

"*Awwww.*" The sound came again, followed by laboured breathing, as if someone or something was finding it difficult to draw breath.

Carefully, silently, Lucy put the cardboard box down on the ground. Then she peered round the tree and, as stealthily as she could, made her way towards the sound, her heart beating like a drum. If it was an animal she was going to help it, but if it was something she didn't want to see, she was going to run like mad in the opposite direction.

Lucy took five steps closer to where the sound had come from, and gave a sudden gasp. There was a man, lying flat on the ground. He was wearing a pair of sturdy brown boots and, tucked into them, a pair of green waterproof trousers. She rounded a tree and gave another gasp. It was Mr Mack, lying flat out, his eyes closed, looking pale and ill.

Before Lucy could even think about Mr

Mack – about what he'd done and how she'd vowed not to be friends with him any more – she'd darted to his side.

"Mr Mack!" Lucy bent over him. "Are you all right?" It was a pretty silly question, she thought, when it was obvious that he wasn't.

His eyelids fluttered. "Is that you, young Lucy?" he said in a voice a little above a whisper.

"Yes. It's me," Lucy said. "Have you fallen, Mr Mack? Broken your leg or something?"

Mr Mack let out another groan. "My left arm," he said. "I fell on it."

Lucy gingerly looked at the arm, which was twisted underneath Mr Mack's body. "How long have you been here? I'll run and get an ambulance, shall I?" Lucy got to her feet, ready to sprint off home, but Mr Mack gave a low moan of distress.

"No. Wait."

Lucy crouched down again. "What is it? Is there something else I can do?"

"I'm a diabetic," Mr Mack whispered. "I've got sugar diabetes. I didn't have my lunch today and I need to eat something sugary straight away. I'm too weak to move."

Lucy frantically patted her pockets, searching for a biscuit or a piece of

55

chocolate in one of them. There was nothing. "Shall I run and get you something?"

"Yes, please," Mr Mack said weakly. "My back door's open. You'll find a packet of glucose sweets on the side. And ring the ambulance while you're there. Tell them where to find me."

Lucy was just about to run off when she remembered Trouble, and went back to the tree to pick up his box. She put it down beside Mr Mack. "I'll be as quick as I possibly can," she said, "and in the meantime there's a piglet to keep you company."

Mr Mack nodded weakly. "I like piglets," he whispered.

Fifteen minutes later, Lucy had run all the way to Mr Mack's farm, found the glucose tablets, phoned for help and was back again.

"The ambulance man said they'd get as

close to here as possible," she panted, breaking open the packet of tablets. "I'm to listen for them and go out in the lane and wave when I see them." She pushed a tablet into Mr Mack's mouth. "I know about diabetes," she said, "because a girl in my class has it. The teacher has to keep snacks in her bag all the time – just in case."

Mr Mack didn't speak, just sucked, chewed and swallowed until he'd eaten half the glucose tablets. Only then did he give a deep sigh. He adjusted his position on the ground slightly, wincing as he moved his arm. "I'll be all right now, lass," he said. "I was frightened for a while there, though. If I went into a diabetic coma I could have lain here all weekend and not been found. I would have died, for certain."

"Oh, no – someone would have noticed you were missing," Lucy began.

Mr Mack shook his head. "My house-keeper's got the week off. No one knows I came out for a walk down here."

"Well, it's just as well I was coming to hide Trouble then, wasn't it?" Lucy said. Although she was still cross with Mr Mack and couldn't understand why he was selling his farm, he'd helped her out so many times in the past that she couldn't help but be pleased that she had a chance to help *him* now.

"Trouble. That's his name, is it?"

Lucy nodded and told Mr Mack how she'd got him, and about the inspector and her mum, and how she'd decided to hide Trouble in one of the coops.

"Let's see him properly, then," Mr Mack said. "I started off as a pig farmer, you know. Very intelligent animals, pigs."

Lucy lifted a squealing Trouble out of his box. "I know," she said. "We've done something about them at school."

When Trouble was on the ground he stopped squealing and looked down at Mr Mack. He seemed to be studying the old man, head on one side.

Mr Mack chuckled weakly. "He's a saucy little chap! D'you know, while you were off getting help I was talking to him in his box there, and I swear he answered me. I'd speak and then he'd grunt in reply. Very funny!"

As they watched, Trouble ran a few steps and sniffed around in the leaf mould on the ground. Burrowing his nose deep in it, he unearthed an acorn, tossed it free of the earth and then, squealing, ran after it.

They both laughed and Lucy went to pick him up – and then heard the *nee-naw* of an ambulance.

"That didn't take long," Mr Mack said in relief.

"I'll go and tell them where you are," Lucy said, putting Trouble back in his box.

Mr Mack raised his head a little. "I want to thank you, lass," he said. "Thanks for everything."

Lucy smiled, embarrassed. "That's OK," she said, thinking that she couldn't possibly say anything about the housing estate *now*. She patted the old man on his good arm. "You'll be all right now, Mr Mack."

Chapter Six

"And then," Lucy said breathlessly, "the ambulance arrived—"

"I heard it going by!" her mum said, wide-eyed.

". . . and I ran out to the lane and waved so it could get as close to us as possible. They helped Mr Mack up and put a sling thing round his arm, and then they put him on a stretcher and put him in the ambulance and took him away!"

"Well!" her mum said. Suddenly her attention was drawn to a movement outside the kitchen window and she pulled an anguished face. "Oh my goodness, there's Mr Bourne back again! He was just having a word with your dad about Mr Mack's plans and the development scheme. He says he'll still review us for this year, thank goodness. Now, Lucy, love, can you lay the table for me – don't forget the soup spoons – and then get rid of the dogs. You can tie them up outside somewhere. Then go outside and pick some flowers from the hedges, find a vase in the pantry to put them in and – oh, take Kerry with you and get her from under my feet, will you?"

Lucy raised her eyebrows. "Anything else?" she asked cheekily.

"Get along with you!" her mum said. "And remember to chat nicely over supper and *smile* at Mr Bourne so he can see how very friendly and charming we are!"

*

When Lucy came back with Kerry in one hand and a bunch of poppies, cornflowers and cow parsley in the other, her mum and dad were chatting to Mr Bourne in the yard. Her dad was saying something about having a few young animals around the farm all year to amuse any visiting children, and her mum was saying that there was nothing town children liked better than bottle-feeding a lamb.

"Of course, you would apply very strict hygiene rules after any association with animals?" Mr Bourne said.

"Oh, absolutely," Julie Tremayne said earnestly. "I always make sure our visitors scrub their hands after animal contact. We know how important that is." She turned to beam at Lucy. "What lovely flowers! Mr Bourne, you've met our elder daughter, of course."

"I have indeed," Mr Bourne said, nodding at Lucy. Heart in her mouth, Lucy hoped he wasn't going to mention the "puppy".

"Shall we go inside? Supper's just about ready," Julie Tremayne said, and she led the way into the house.

As they went through the boot lobby (clean cushions had magically appeared in the dogs' baskets, Lucy noticed) there was a flutter and a squawk as a fat, speckled chicken fluttered down from the hat rack.

Mr Bourne gave a shout of surprise. "What on earth's that?"

"Cheep, cheep chicken!" Kerry said.

"What's a hen doing in here?" Lucy's dad asked. "Chase her outside, will you, Lucy?"

"That's Freckles," Lucy said. "I hope she's not going broody again and hiding her eggs."

"I especially hope she hasn't deposited any on our hat rack," Lucy's mum said. Turning, she almost slipped on a small pile of chicken droppings. She gave a tiny shriek. "Wipe that up, Tim, would you darling?" she said, smiling fixedly at her husband.

Lucy put the flowers in a vase, then went to get some cushions for Kerry to sit on. Recently Kerry had been refusing to go in her high chair, demanding an ordinary chair like everyone else. Being on an ordinary chair, however, meant her head

hardly came up to the table top, so she had to be balanced on a pile of cushions.

After sorting Kerry out, Lucy sat down herself. She was dying to tell her dad all about Mr Mack but, being a little worried that it might start him off about the new estate, she thought she'd better leave it until later.

All was going according to plan. Mr and Mrs Walker came in, greeted everyone, and took their places at the table. Lucy's mum put a big china tureen on the table and served the soup, which was vegetable. Everyone tucked in and said how tasty it was.

"Marvellous," Mr Bourne enthused. "I can always tell home-made soup. It's got real substance to it, not like the shop-bought variety. The vegetables are from the garden, are they?"

Lucy's mum nodded. "The brown rolls are home-made too," she said, passing a basket of bread. She adjusted the bib around Kerry's neck. "When people come on a farm holiday they want real, nourishing meals. I try to make sure everything is home-made."

"Your meals are absolutely first class!" Mr Walker said. He was a male version of Mrs Walker – plump, with wiry grey hair and red-veined cheeks.

"They certainly are. We'll be going home a lot fatter than when we came!" Mrs Walker joined in.

The Tremayne family smiled at each other, rather pleased with themselves. Suddenly though they heard barking in the yard, and Podger raced straight through the open back door, closely chased by Roger. Before anyone could shout or make a move towards either dog, Podger had run towards the Aga and leapt up at an apple pie which had been taken out of the oven. The pie tin crashed to the floor, breaking the pie into pieces, and Roger immediately carried off a quarter of it.

As the dogs ran out again and disappeared somewhere to squabble over the pie, Lucy's mum just sat there with her mouth open, looking from Mr Bourne to the Aga and back again.

"What are those dogs doing racing about, Lucy?" her mum asked quietly.

"I thought I told you to tie them up somewhere."

"I did! They must have broken free."

"*Naughty* doggies!" Kerry said.

Mr Bourne took another spoonful of soup. "Ah well," he said, "this is still pretty good soup."

Kerry gave a shriek of glee. "Super soup!" She wriggled, fell off her cushions and crashed her soup spoon flat into her bowl so that a splatter of vegetable soup went up in the air and all over Mr Bourne. She lay on the floor crying as Mrs Tremayne ran round to pick her up and cuddle her.

Lucy cringed, looking round at the stricken faces of her mum and dad. The inspection was going all wrong. Today was not going to be a good day to bring up the subject of piglets . . .

*

"I don't know *what* you must think of us," Lucy's mum said, when they were sitting around the table after the meal, Mr and Mrs Walker having gone off for an evening stroll down the lanes. "Everything seemed to go haywire this evening!"

Mr Bourne laughed and reached for his cup of coffee. "Please don't worry," he said. "I think it's absolutely lovely here. You've got a real family atmosphere, and that's what the holidaymakers are after. They've chosen to stay on a farm – they don't want a posh hotel with regulation meals and everything stiff and formal."

"I suppose so." Lucy's mum tried to raise a smile.

"So – are you going to give us a good rating?" Lucy's dad asked jovially. "Or are we to be in the no-crown category? Avoid this place at all costs – low-flying chickens, dogs running wild and soup everywhere."

Mr Bourne laughed. Lucy noticed he had a speck of what looked like carrot on his bald head. "Of course not! As I said, anyone who comes here will be wanting a taste of farm living – and that's what they'll get. You're surrounded by beautiful countryside, you've got comfortable rooms, access to animals for the children – and I love the little piglet, by the way!"

Lucy, who'd been about to clear the table, stopped dead. He'd seen Trouble! Her mum and dad stared at Mr Bourne, frowning.

"What piglet?" Lucy's mum asked.

"Ha ha!" Mr Bourne laughed. "That's your standing joke, is it? You try and pretend it's a puppy."

"We don't keep pigs!" said Lucy's dad. "Never have done."

"Kids *love* piglets, don't they," Mr Bourne went on, "especially since that film. They—" Mr Bourne stopped and looked at Lucy's dad hard. "*What*?"

"We don't keep pigs," Lucy's dad repeated.

"Mainly because I can't stand them," said Lucy's mum.

Mr Bourne looked at Lucy, puzzled. "But your daughter had one earlier this afternoon. First of all he was in a cardboard box. And then I saw him running along the worktop. She was trying to pretend to Mrs Walker that it was a puppy. Good joke, I thought."

Lucy's mum drew her breath in sharply. "A pig! In here? Running along my worktop?"

Lucy's dad laid a heavy hand on Lucy's shoulder. "OK, Miss Tremayne. I think you'd better explain."

Lucy looked at her mum and dad and gulped. She took a deep breath. "Well, it's like this. You see . . ."

Chapter Seven

"I just didn't know what to do with him when I'd won him," Lucy tried to explain again. The family, with Mr Bourne, who was about to leave, were standing in the farmyard. "I mean, I didn't expect to actually win or I wouldn't have gone in for the competition in the first place."

"So where is he now, this piglet of yours?" her dad asked.

"He's hidden in one of Mr Mack's pheasant coops," Lucy said. She was dying to giggle but thought she'd better not. "D'you want to see him?" She shot a look at her mum. "He's gorgeous, he really is."

Mr Bourne coughed. "I can vouch for that," he said. "And as I say, the kids will love him. I think he'd be an asset to the farm."

"Hmm," Lucy's dad said, while her mum gave Lucy a familiar *just you wait, young lady* look.

Mr Bourne pulled a notebook out of his pocket and jotted something down. "I shouldn't really tell you this, it's supposed to come in writing, but I'll be giving you top marks for a bed and breakfast farm. In this year's guide you'll be classified as four crowns."

"Wow!" Lucy said.

Her dad was beaming.

"That's marvellous," said her mum.

"And all that remains is for me to thank you for a delicious – and interesting – meal," Mr Bourne went on. As he turned to open his car door, Lucy noticed that as well as the piece of carrot on his head, he now had a cut-out green felt elephant of Kerry's stuck to the seat of his trousers.

The family said their goodbyes and waved until Mr Bourne had driven down the lane and out of sight, then Lucy's mum collapsed over the five-bar gate.

"Run me a bath, someone," she said. "I'm absolutely shattered!"

"What a day!" her dad said.

"You haven't heard the half of it, Dad," Lucy said. "I've still got to tell you all about Mr Mack."

"What's he been up to now?" her dad grumbled. "Don't tell me – he's sold his place and we're having Disneyland Devon here."

"No – of course not!" Lucy said, but her dad wouldn't be stopped.

"I mean, it's all very well having the

best rating for Bed and Breakfast," he said, "but who's going to come here when we're surrounded by streets, houses and betting shops? Mr Bourne was very dubious about people still wanting to come here."

"I was just on my way to—" Lucy tried again.

"I mean, it'll ruin the whole area. Nothing will be the same."

"I tell you what," Lucy's mum came to the rescue. "I'll tell your dad about how you saved Mr Mack while we get Kerry ready for bed – and *you* go and get this piglet of yours."

Lucy brightened up. "Are you sure?"

Lucy's dad licked his lips. "Pork chops – my favourite."

"Dad!"

"Now, you know he doesn't mean that. Go and get the piglet and we'll try and decide what to do with it." Lucy's mum shuddered. "But don't bring it anywhere near me."

"*Whee! Whee!*"

An hour later, Trouble could be seen tripping daintily across the kitchen of Hollybrook Farm, his curly tail bobbing behind him. He'd spotted a crust of bread that had been dropped by Kerry earlier, and was on his way to eat it.

"Now! Just look at him and tell me he isn't gorgeous!" Lucy said.

Lucy's dad laughed. "Very nice. Pass the apple sauce, someone!"

"Well." Lucy's mum stood in the door-way of the kitchen, poised to run away if Trouble approached her. "I suppose . . . as pigs go . . . he's fairly OK. I mean, I don't exactly feel *threatened* by him."

"As if!" Lucy said.

"But he'll grow, Lucy. In six months' time he'll be a big, enormous, fat pig. He'll

be covered in mud, snuffling in dirt
and . . ." she shuddered, ". . . eating
worms."

"I read in a book that pigs are only dirty
if they live in dirty places," Lucy said
earnestly. "If he has a nice clean, dry sty,
there's no reason why he shouldn't stay
clean and dry himself."

"But what will we *do* with him?" Lucy's
dad said.

"He'll be fun for the children who visit!" Lucy said. "You heard what Mr Bourne said – everyone loves pigs."

"Not everyone," said Lucy's mum darkly.

"And he'll hardly cost us anything because he'll eat scraps."

"Our scraps already get eaten by all your other animals!" Tim Tremayne said.

"Scraps that the other animals leave," said Lucy doggedly.

"And where's he going to live? I can't construct a special sty just for him."

"But . . ." Lucy, stuck for what to say next, nibbled her bottom lip and looked at her parents anxiously. It seemed to be deadlock.

Just then, when they were all standing around the kitchen looking at each other, there was a knock at the door.

Lucy opened it. Mr Mack was standing outside. His left arm was in a sling, but in his right hand he held a big bunch of roses and carnations.

"Oh," Lucy said. "Are you all right?"

Mr Mack nodded rather uneasily. "I'm OK." He coughed. "I might not be very welcome, but can I come in, lass?"

"Of course you can," said Lucy's mum, appearing behind her daughter. She'd known Mr Mack for too long to turn him away.

The old man came into the kitchen and handed the bunch of flowers to Lucy. "These are for you," he said. "I reckon I would have died if you hadn't come along."

Lucy went red and mumbled her thanks, hardly knowing what to say.

"Are you all right now?" her dad asked, rather stiffly. "Lucy told us about finding you in the woods."

"I'll be fine," Mr Mack said. "I've just got to be a bit more careful about my diabetes and never go anywhere without a snack in my pocket. And my arm – well, it's quite a small break. Should be mended within six weeks, they say. They plastered me up and brought me home in the ambulance."

"That's good," Lucy said. She glanced up at her mum and dad uncertainly. At any other time, they would have offered Mr Mack a drink or something to eat – or at least asked him to sit down – but things were different now.

Suddenly, Trouble streaked through the kitchen, ran out into the hall and squealed loudly at Podger's basket. Podger woke and looked at the piglet in surprise. "Woof!" he went, and everyone laughed.

"So there he is!" Mr Mack said. "There's Trouble."

"We were just deciding what to do with him when you knocked," Lucy's mum said.

Mr Mack nodded slowly. "I may be able to offer you a solution there. If you agree."

Lucy and her parents looked at him.

"I've come here for two reasons, you see. Firstly to thank Lucy for helping me, and secondly to tell you that I won't be selling my farm after all."

A huge grin slowly spread over Lucy's dad's face. "Well, that *is* good news!"

"You won't?" Lucy asked, hardly daring to believe it.

"Why ever not?" said Lucy's mum.

Lucy's dad pulled out a chair for him. "Take a seat, Mr Mack."

"Cup of tea?" Lucy's mum offered.

Mr Mack sat down heavily, resting his plastered arm on the table. "It's like this," he said. "When young Lucy left me with Trouble in the woods, I got to chatting to him and thinking. And then, while I was hours in the hospital waiting to be plastered up, I thought some more."

Everyone waited while Mr Mack gazed into the distance. "I used to be a pig farmer, you see, back in the old days. Good animals, they are. Clever animals. Tidy profit too."

"Go on," said Lucy's dad.

"Pigs are intelligent. Much more interesting than sheep. And what I was thinking this afternoon, was that farming isn't just about making money. It's about enjoying yourself and living in a good environment among" – he glanced up at them – "good people. Well, to cut a long story short – what I decided was that instead of selling up I'd like to turn my farm around. Make some changes. Sell my sheep and keep pigs again."

"Wow!" Lucy said.

"Brilliant idea!" said her dad.

Lucy's mum didn't say anything, and when Lucy looked to see why, she saw that her eyes were full of tears. Lucy's hand crept into hers.

"And in honour of young Trouble here being one of the reasons I changed my mind, I'd like to offer him the distinction of being the first pig on my new farm," Mr Mack said. "If you're in agreement, Trouble would be my number one pig – a permanent resident at Mack's Piggeries!"

"Well, I think I can say that's fine by

us," Lucy's dad said, still grinning broadly.

"Wow!" Lucy made a grab for Trouble. "Hear that, Trouble?" she said, holding him up. "You're going to be number one pig. Isn't that just absolutely . . . absolutely . . ." she searched her mind for a good enough word. "Isn't that *pigtastic*!"

LUCY'S FARM 2
Lucy's Donkey Rescue

When Lucy meets a poor neglected donkey on the beach, she is desperate to help him. His horrible owner is so cruel.

Lucy knows that her parents will never agree to keeping another animal on the farm. Can Donald, a very clever donkey, prove that Hollybrook really does need him?

LUCY'S FARM 3
Lucy's Badger Cub

Lucy and her friend Beth enjoy watching the badgers in the woods. They are horrified to find one day that all the badgers have gone – except for one little cub.

But there are more mysteries down in the woods. Someone has been living in the old ruined cottage. Can Lucy discover what is going on – and save her little badger cub?